Franklin Feels at Home

Kids Can Press

FRANKLIN and Bear were best friends. They loved spending time together. So they were excited to find out that Franklin was going to stay at Bear's place for two whole days while his parents and Harriet were out of town.

Franklin was looking forward to the sleepover, but he was also a little worried about being away from home for so long.

"Thanks for having Franklin over, Bear,"
said Mrs. Turtle.

"No problem," said Bear. "We're going to
have lots of fun!"

Franklin gave his parents and Harriet
a hug and said goodbye. He sighed as he
watched them leave.

"Come on, Franklin," said Bear. "Let's go
inside and have some dinner."

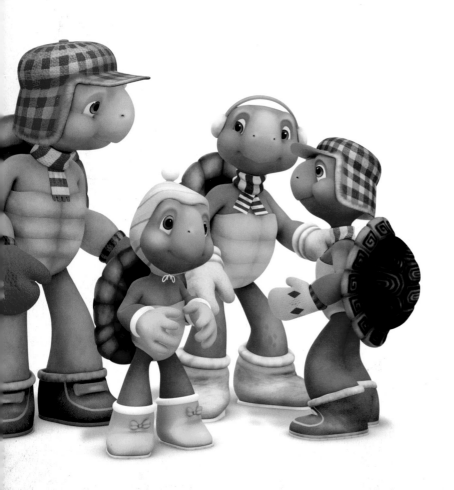

Dr. Bear made honey crepes for dinner.

Franklin looked down at his plate and gulped. "Friday night is lettuce casserole night at our house," he said.

Franklin took a bite. He chewed very slowly and then swallowed.
"Hey, this is good!" he said.
"Thank you, Franklin," said Dr. Bear, smiling.

"What do you want to do tomorrow?" Bear asked later that night.

"Let's build a snow dragon," said Franklin.

"Awesome idea!" said Bear. "Let's go to sleep now so we can get up early and start building."

Bear turned out the lights. Soon he started to snore.
    But Franklin couldn't sleep. Bear's room was very dark, and the wind made the house creak.

"Yippee!" said Bear, as the boys raced outside the next morning. "Let's get started on our snow dragon!"

Franklin and Bear rolled three giant snowballs and lined them up. Then they added pinecones for the dragon's snout, rocks for its eyes and sticks for its antlers and arms.

"What do you think?" asked Bear when they were done.

"Cool-io!" said Franklin.

"You must be hungry from all your hard work," Mr. Bear said when the boys sat down for lunch.

"Starved!" said Franklin. He took a small bite of his sandwich and frowned. "Honey?" he asked.

"My favorite!" said Bear.
"My mom usually makes me lettuce sandwiches," said Franklin.
"I'm sorry, Franklin," said Mr. Bear. "We're all out of lettuce."
"That's okay," said Franklin. "This is good, too."

After lunch, Franklin and Bear went back outside.

"Let's make the snow dragon even bigger!" said Bear.

"Great idea!" said Franklin.

Franklin got to work rolling snowballs. Soon his mittens were soaking wet.

Bear went inside and came back out with a pair of his old mittens. "Try these on," he said.

"They're a bit big ..." said Franklin.

"Let's give the dragon some wings!" said Bear.

"And some teeth!" said Franklin.

Franklin tried to attach a stick to the snow dragon for a wing, but Bear's big mittens kept getting in his way. Then he tried to help Bear put carrots in the dragon's mouth for teeth. That didn't work either.

Franklin pulled Bear's mittens off and threw them down in the snow.

"What's the matter?" asked Bear.

"I'm just not used to things around here," said Franklin. "And I miss my family. I wish they could be here with me."

"Hmmm … maybe they can," said Bear.

Franklin watched as Bear rolled some more big snowballs. "What are those for?" he asked.

"We're going to make snow *turtles*!" said Bear.

Franklin smiled. "That's a great idea," he said, putting his own mittens back on.

Together, the boys stacked the snowballs and carved them into the shapes of Franklin's family.

"It's almost like they're really here," Franklin said, as he added a bow to the top of the snow Harriet's head.

As Franklin and Bear walked into the house for dinner, Franklin smelled something delicious.

"Who wants lettuce casserole?" Mr. Bear asked.

"Mmmm," said Franklin. "That smells as good as my mom's!"
"It should," Dr. Bear said with a laugh. "She gave us the recipe!"

"Look what I found," said Bear later that night.

"Sam!" said Franklin. "Where did you find him?"

"I accidentally knocked over your bag, and he fell out," said Bear.

"My mom must have packed him," said Franklin, smiling. "She always knows just what I need."

"And I found this old flashlight," said Bear. "I thought you might want it in case it gets too dark in my room."

"Thanks, Bear," said Franklin. "I guess you know just what I need, too."

Franklin lay down and shone his flashlight on Sam. Then he closed his eyes and fell fast asleep.

The next day, the Turtles came back from their trip.

Mrs. Turtle gave Franklin a big hug. "We missed you," she said.

"I missed you, too," said Franklin. "But thanks to Bear and his family, I felt right at home."